MR. BADGER AND MRS. FOX #6

THE WILD CAT

Brigitte LUCIANI & Eve THARLET

Graphic Universe™ • Minneapolis

Story by Brigitte Luciani
Art by Eve Tharlet
Translation by Nathan Sacks

First American edition published in 2018 by Graphic Universe™.
Published by arrangement with MEDIATOON LICENSING—France.

Monsieur Blaireau et Madame Renarde
6/Le Chat Sauvage

www.dargaud.com

Graphic Universe™
A division of Lerner Publishing Group, Inc.
241 First Avenue North
Minneapolis, MN 55401 USA

For reading levels and more information, look up this title at www.lernerbooks.com.

Library of Congress Cataloging-in-Publication Data

Names: Luciani, Brigitte, author. | Tharlet, Eve, illustrator. | Sacks, Nathan, translator.
Title: The wild cat / Brigitte Luciani & Eve Tharlet ; translation by Nathan Sacks.
Other titles: Chat sauvage. English
Description: First American edition. | Minneapolis : Graphic Universe, 2018. | Series: Mr. Badger and Mrs. Fox ; #6 | Originally published in France by Dargaud in 2016 under title: Le chat sauvage. | Summary: After watching a performance of a wild cat climbing trees, Ginger the fox decides to learn to climb trees herself, but when she is criticized for not behaving like a fox, she leaves her blended family behind in search of other foxes. | Identifiers: LCCN 2017044305 (print) | LCCN 2017058394 (ebook) | ISBN 9781541500884 (eb pdf) | ISBN 9781541500860 (lb : alk. paper) | ISBN 9781541500877 (pb : alk. paper)
Subjects: LCSH: Graphic novels. | CYAC: Graphic novels. | Self-acceptance—Fiction. | Stepfamilies—Fiction. | Foxes—Fiction. | Badgers—Fiction.
Classification: LCC PZ7.7.L83 (ebook) | LCC PZ7.7.L83 Wi 2018 (print) | DDC 741.5/973—dc23

LC record available at https://lccn.loc.gov/2017044305

Manufactured in the United States of America
1-43757-33617-3/9/2018

Your turn, Grub!
Okay, let's go! Who am I?

Do you live in the water?
No.
Do you have legs for walking?
Yes, Ginger!

And wings for flying?
Also yes, Bristle.
So... who am I?

You're a little badger who likes to play "Who am I?"!
Ha ha ha!

Hello! We have a question...

Us too! Who are you?
You may call us the Fabulous Genettes.

Gennifer...
Gena...
And Genevieve.

We're looking for a place to put on a show for tonight.
What show?

A show for the Great Sylvester!
The WILD CAT!

HERE?
Yeah!!
You can set up in the clearing. We'll show you.
Cool!

I've never heard of this Sylvester.
He's great—you'll see!

But what's the difference between a normal cat and a wild cat?

They're not AT ALL the same!
But they look the same.

Not even! A wild cat is much stronger.
And bigger.
And flashy!
Pfft.

Also, you can tell a wild cat by the rings on his tail.
HEY! You heard?

Sylvester's doing two shows, one today and one tomorrow.
We're seeing him tonight. How about you?
Us too!
Come on, we'll tell our folks!

What about our game? It's not done yet.
We haven't figured out who Grub was!
We'll finish another time.

Ladybug.
Huh?!

You did it! Berry, you just won! How did you figure out who I am?

Ladybug!

Where do we sit?
Front and center!
It's quite comfortable.
Not for me. I need to make this hole a bit bigger...
I can't see, Mom!
Huuusshhh!
When does it start?
Ooh!
Ah!
Oooh!
Aah!
Ooh!
Ah!
Oooh!
Hello, adoring public. Let's give a warm welcome to SYLVESTER!
The great...
The incredible...
The magnificent...

WILD CAT!
Aaaaaah!
Ooooh!

HOORAY!
Bravo!
Bravo!
Awesome!
He's so good!
I'm impressed.

Aaaaaah!
Ooooh!

Sylvesterrr!
An autograph? Please?
Clear the way!
We're gonna try to meet him!
Okay. We're going home with Berry—there are too many fans!

See ya later!

That cat has class.
When I grow up, I want to be like him!
Sure, Ginger. There's just one problem. You don't know how to climb trees!

Says who? I've never tried.

Me neither.
Hee hee, I think I know why!

Ginger!

Stop, you crazy fox!

Don't ruin my concentration.

What is she doing?
Not losing her concentration.
And we're her safety net!

Careful...
Don't fall, little sis!

I DID IT!

SHE DID IT!

That fox thinks for herself, doesn't she?

She climbed up the tree like a snail, and now she's happy.

She won't be so happy when she tries to climb down.

Stop teasing me! I need to train, that's all.

Sylvester, did you hear what the redhead said?
What do you think?

Now what do we have here?

A little fox?
Hello!

You know what I think about little foxes who go climbing up trees?

I think it's RIDICULOUS.

Reee-diculous!

That's Ginger, the daughter of your friend Mr. Fox.
Oh, really? So Basil's little girl thinks she's a squirrel. How delightful.
Ha!
Ha!
Ha!

What are you doing with those badgers?
I live with them.

Pff! It doesn't matter.
I pity your father.

He must be ashamed of you!

Ginger!
Come down!

Bottom
first!

If you could
avoid falling, we'd
appreciate it!

Plop!

Thanks!

You met Sylvester
up there!
What did he
say?
Drop it!
I'm tired. I'm
going home.

?!

You're still in bed, Ginger? What's going on?

When will Papa come see me?
I'm not sure. You know him. He never tells us first.

Do you think he's angry with me?
Of course not! Why do you ask?
It's been a long time since he visited...

I know...but I'm sure he'll come soon.
He never goes too long without visiting.

And now, **HOP UP!** The others are already out playing!

Ginger, finally!
Want to show us your moves from yesterday?

Eh.
What are you two doing?
We're building a slide!

Well, it's going to be a wild ride for you badgers.
But **SUPER BORING** for a fox. Is that it?

Sorry, guys. I think it's better if I hang out by myself today.

INJER!
No, Berry, stay there! You're a little badger. Your place is with your brothers.

My place. Where's MY place?
I wonder if I AM a real fox.
It's no use talking with Mama. She's like me. She lives with badgers too.

I should talk with other foxes. But where do I find them?
I'll have to leave our territory.

Well, definitely not at home anymore.

It won't be long until they find me. I just have to wait.

Well, hello, little one!
What are you doing here?

Visiting?

By yourself?
Yes.
You're not very careful.
I hear that a lot.

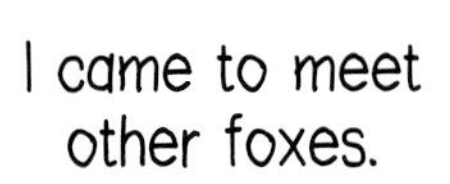
I came to meet other foxes.

Then you're in luck.
If you're here to find foxes, foxes you will find!

We have a visitor, Ma!

Oh, and who's this charming young fox?
My name's Ginger.

Welcome to our foxhole, Ginger!
Hello.
Not from around here?
Are you lost?
You must be tired. Sit down!

It looks nice with your white hair!
Where are you from?
Why do you have a split ear?
Who are you?
Have some locusts, Ginger.

They're good, right?
Mmm!

Let's take a deep breath, everybody.
Pa!

So you came to see other foxes?
They aren't enough fun, the ones near you?
Ha ha ha!

There's only my mama and me.
You both live alone?
No, no, we're not alone.

We live with badgers.
HUH?

You swept right by that part!
Let's not be rude...
But, Pa, she's the one saying weird things.

I said: LET'S NOT BE RUDE!

Plenty of foxes share their burrows with badgers. I did it myself when I was younger.
HUH?

And I really liked it!
Me too.

Meanwhile...
I wonder where she went.
There's the Genettes. They might know something.

Hello! Have you seen Ginger?
Who's that again?
The little fox who lives with them.

Oh, that one. She's more **BADGER** than fox!
Ha!
Ha!
Ha!
Ha!
Ha!
Ha!

Have you seen Ginger—
YES or **NO?**

Yeah, we saw her.
We saw her running.
Where?
Far.

Far from badgers!
Ha! Ha! Ha!

Grrgh!

Ha ha ha! A badger trying to catch a genet.
How ridiculous!
As ridiculous as a fox who tries to climb trees.

Ha!
Ha!
Ha!
Hey! Ginger succeeded! She climbed a tree!

What bullies!
I despise them!
Why does Sylvester hang out with them?

We have to teach them a lesson.
But they're too fast for us!
Don't worry. I have an idea.

Want to help?
My pleasure!

Bye, Ginger!
See you later!

Can I ask you guys a question?
Go ahead. Don't be shy.

Am I a real fox to you?
HUH?
She said, "Am I a real fox?"

I heard, but why is she asking? It's a weird question, right?
So what? She has a right to ask weird questions.

Ha ha ha! Thanks! I think you answered my question.
Oh yeah?

Well, so much the better. We're at the edge of our territory.
Look, over there!

Papa!

Looks like she knows him.
Yep! "Mission: Save the Girl" accomplished.

You made some fox friends?
Eighteen of them! And I have lots of other things to tell you.

You see?
Clever!

You are your father's daughter.
Why do you say that? Did you climb trees too?
Sometimes.

I like to watch the world from above.
Dad...
Are you proud of me?
YES!
Your friend Sylvester said I'm not normal and that you're ashamed of me because I climb trees like a squirrel and live with badgers.
You're not ashamed of me?
What a crazy idea!
He'll say anything, that Sylvester!
But he's right on one point.
It's true you're not a normal fox.
You're an **EXTRAORDINARY** fox!

Ginger!
Hello, Basil!
We just tried to see the Genettes, but it didn't work out. They're backstage with Sylvester.
What did you want from them?
I'll explain later.
Come with us. Dad wants to talk with Sylvester.
STOP! The public is not allowed in yet!
Relax, Gennifer. Don't you recognize him?

Basil! To what do I owe the honor of this visit?
You owe us an explanation, Sylvester.

I hear you think it's ridiculous when a fox climbs trees?

But it was you, years ago, who taught me how to climb!
That's true.
It was a long time ago.

Sure. Back then, you were not quite THE GREAT WILD CAT.
Hush! Not so loud.

Come this way. We can speak in private.

Now!

SURPRISE!

Aaaaaaaaaaaaaaaah!
SPLASH

I'm soaked!
Noooo!

Ha! Ha! Ha!
What big shots!
They're afraid of water!

Oops.

You weren't supposed to get wet.
Hold still.

I'll dry you off.
Don't bother!

Sylvester, your rings...
They're painted on!?

You're not really a wild cat?

Go ahead, say it!

It's true. I'm just a simple old cat.

I lied to everyone.

Forgive me, Ginger! I wasn't nice to you yesterday.
It's not you who's ridiculous.

It's **ME.**

You try new things. That's brave.
Me, I pretend to be someone I'm not. I'm a coward.

But why don't you say you're a regular cat?

Audiences want spectacle! No one will be satisfied with a plain cat.
The public wants to see someone **EXCEPTIONAL.**

Anyway, I hate cats...
His parents left him in the forest. He grew up alone.
Poor guy!

Everyone thinks that I'm a wild cat. Even the Genettes.
But now...
It's OVER.
If I unmask, what will I become?
I cannot live without my shows. I'm an ARTIST!
Don't worry! We'll keep your secret.
And we'll help you make up for it.
You won't give me up?
No, we swear!
Thank you! You've saved my life as an artist.

So, Ginger, you still want to be like Sylvester?
BRAVO, SYLVESTER!
Oooh!
Aaah!
No thanks! I'm glad to be a simple little fox.
A fox who lives with badgers.
And who sometimes does strange things?
And so what? So much the better, right?
Yipeeeeeee!
Yeah! So much the better!